This
Harry
book belongs to

....

For Josh Hughes who really
knows about robots
I.W.

For Martin
A.R.

PUFFIN BOOKS

Published by the Penguin Group: London, New York, Australia, Canada, India, Ireland, New Zealand and South Africa
Penguin Books Ltd, Registered Offices: 80 Strand, London WC2R 0RL, England

puffinbooks.com

First published in hardback by David and Charles Children's Books 2000
First published in paperback by Gullane Children's Books 2001
Published in Puffin Books 2003
Published in this edition 2005
Reissued 2008
1 3 5 7 9 10 8 6 4 2
Text copyright © Ian Whybrow, 2000
Illustrations copyright © Adrian Reynolds, 2000
All rights reserved
The moral right of the author and illustrator has been asserted
Made and printed in China
ISBN 978–0–141–50074–4

Harry
and the
Robots

Ian Whybrow and Adrian Reynolds

PUFFIN

It was a shock for Harry
when his robot fell over.
It was just doing a nice march
and suddenly its lights went out.

Harry heard Nan coughing in the yard,
so he ran out to show her.

Some of the robot's batteries had leaked onto its wires.
They put him in a parcel and sent him to the robot hospital.
"They'll know how to mend him," Nan said.

Harry wanted to make another robot to play with while he waited for his marching robot to come back.
Nan said, "Good idea. We'll use my best scissors if you like."
They laid the things ready on the table.

But they never got started.
Mum made Nan go to bed,
her cough was so bad.

When Harry woke up the next morning, there was no Nan. The ambulance had come in the night. She had to go into hospital, Mum said, for her bad chest.

That day, Sam watched
TV a lot.

Harry started making a robot all by himself.
He wanted to use Nan's best scissors. Nan had said he could.
But Sam said, "No! Those are Nan's!"

That was why Harry threw his Stegosaurus at her.

Mum took him to settle down.
She said he could use Nan's best scissors if
Nan had said so, but only while she was
watching. He had to be very careful
though, because they were sharp.

Harry worked hard
all morning . . .

. . . until there was a new robot. A special one.

    Harry taught it marching. He taught it talking.

    But most of all he taught it blasting.

The robot said,

"Ha - Lo Har - Ree.

Have - you - got - a - cough?

BLAAAST!"

BLAAAST!

The hospital was big but they found Nan in there.

Mum said Sam and Harry had
to wait outside Nan's room.
They waved through the window
but Nan did not open her eyes.

Sam and Mum whispered with the doctor. So Harry slipped into the room – just him and the special robot.

He put the special robot by Nan.
The robot said,
  "Ha - Lo - Nan.
      Have - you - got - a - cough?"
She opened one eye. It winked.
The robot said,
  "I - will - blast - your - cough.
      BLAAAST!"

That was when Mum ran in saying – "Harry! No!"
But the doctor said not to worry, it was fine.
A robot would be a nice helper for Nan.

That evening, Harry was very busy.

He joined . . .

he stuck . . .

he painted and . . .

Harry made five more
special robots to look
after Nan.

The robots guarded Nan.
They marched for her.
They blasted her cough.
And soon she was better.

Nan came home and unpacked her things.
"You're a good looker-afterer," she whispered.
"And my special robots," said Harry.
"Oh yes, them too," said Nan.
"I'd like to keep them by me, do you mind?"
Harry did not mind at all.

Nan went out into the yard to see how
the chickens were getting on.
They were just fine.

That afternoon a parcel arrived. It was the marching robot, back from the robot hospital. His light went on and he did a nice march – good as new.